HANDS-ON HISTORY

PROJECTS ABOUT

The American Revolution

Marian Broida

Marshall Cavendish
Benchmark

New York

Acknowledgments

Thanks to the following individuals for their assistance: Ed Ayres, Historian, Yorktown Victory Center; Marc Brier, park ranger, Valley Forge National Historical Park; Mark Nichipor, park ranger, Minuteman National Historical Park; Anna Coxe Toogood, historian, Independence National Historic Park; staff at Boston National Historical Park; Dr. David Kleit; and Dr. Christine Swager. And for help in testing the activities, thanks to Shaina and Rachel Andres, Lynn Chapman, Carolyn Cohen, Jesse Lieberman, Jacob Mayer, and Beatrice Misher.

The conversation on page 12 is adapted from a conversation on pages 187–88 of *The Boston Massacre*, Hiller B. Zobel, New York: W. W. Norton, 1970.

The recipe for stewed pears is adapted from *The Art of Cookery Made Plain and Easy, by a Lady*, 1747 edition, Hannah Glasse, Devon, England: Prospect Books, 1995.

Marshall Cavendish Benchmark
99 White Plains Road
Tarrytown, NY 10591-9001
www.marshallcavendish.us

Library of Congress Cataloging-in-Publication Data

Broida, Marian.
  Projects about the American Revolution / by Marian Broida.
      p. cm. -- (Hands-on history)
Includes bibliographical references and index.
Summary: "Includes social studies projects taken from the Revolutionary
War"--Provided by publisher.
  ISBN 0-7614-1981-0
  1. United States--Social life and customs--1775-1783--Activity
programs--Juvenile literature. 2. United States--History--Revolution,
1775-1783--Study and teaching--Activity programs--Juvenile literature. I.
Title. II. Series.

E163.B855 2005
973.3--dc22

2004027499

Maps and illustrations by Rodica Prato

Title Page: Colonists chase British soldiers across a bridge at the Battle of Concord
Photo research by Joan Meisel

Cover photo: Bettmann/Corbis
Corbis: Bettmann, 6, 7, 11, 12; Joseph Sohm/Visions of America, 43.
Getty Images: MPI, 16; Hulton Archive, 40, 41. *North Wind Picture Archives*: 18, 22, 28, 32.

Printed in China

135642

Contents

⁓

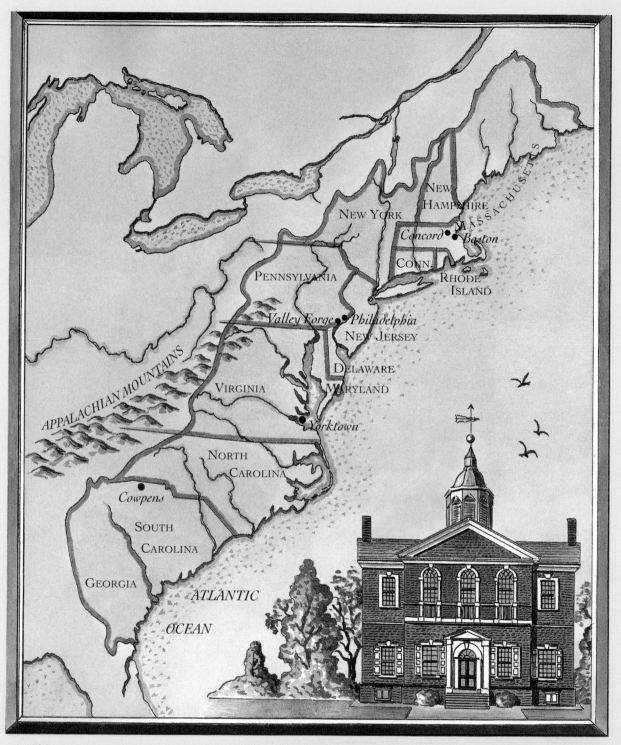

This map shows some of the places mentioned in this book. Key events of the American Revolution took place in these spots.

1

Introduction

What was life like during the American Revolution? Take a trip back in time and meet people who lived in America when the **colonies** were breaking away from Britain. You will join a **loyalist** family worrying over the tea in Boston Harbor, a **patriot** doctor at Valley Forge, a British drummer at the Battle of Yorktown and more.

People worked hard during the revolutionary period. Men, women, and children grew crops, made clothes, and did what was needed to survive. Soldiers battled, often barefoot and hungry.

With this book, you will experience places and events during the time leading up to American independence: Boston on the day of the Boston Massacre; Concord on the first day of the war; Cowpens, South Carolina, during a major American victory. You will make a hat, a flag, and a drum; prepare stewed pears; and create a medical kit. You will feel the passion in the crowd as the brand-new Declaration of Independence is read aloud. Step back in time, and try your hand at history!

The battle of Lexington was the first battle in the Revolutionary War.

2

The Loyalists

In 1765, although many colonists wished for independence from Britain, quite a few others still supported British rule. Those who were loyal to the king were the loyalists or **Tories**. Some Tories worked for the British government. Others were ordinary farmers or working people—sometimes relatives of patriots.

Angry about the **Stamp Act** and other laws they believed to be unfair, mobs of patriots attacked Tories' homes and businesses, and sometimes the Tories themselves. A number of loyalists were **tarred and feathered**. In March 1776 the British took a thousand Boston Tories to safety in Canada. Other loyalists remained in the colonies, especially in the South. When the Americans won the war, many Tories fled to Canada or Britain.

Boston Tea Party. Boston residents, dressed in blankets and pretending to be Indians, dumped tea from three British ships in Boston Harbor on the evening of December 16, 1773.

Stamping Paper

Philadelphia: September 16, 1765

Your father, a carpenter, is putting on his coat. "I'm going out to protect a man named Hughes," he says. "I hear there's a mob gathering to attack him for supporting the Stamp Act."

"Isn't he the one distributing the stamped paper?" asks your mother.

"That's right. The Stamp Act says we all need to pay extra for this paper, and we have to use it. The extra money goes to the British government. They didn't let the colonists vote on the Stamp Act. Most of us think it a very bad idea, but the British gave us no choice."

"But Benjamin," your mother says, "if you don't support the Stamp Act, why are you protecting Hughes?"

"Because no one should be the victim of a mob," he answers.

You will need:

- newspaper
- fine sandpaper if needed
- block of wood (balsa or other), about 3–4 inches per side, from a craft or hardware store
- pencil
- 1 sheet of tracing paper
- scissors
- screwdriver (slot head)
- 1 sheet of flexible craft foam (such as Foamies), about $1/16$ of an inch (2 millimeters) thick
- masking tape
- paintbrush
- acrylic or tempera paint, one or more colors
- jar of water
- several sheets of scrap paper
- plain unlined paper
- damp paper towels

1. Spread out the newspaper on your work surface. Sand the block of wood over the paper if it has rough spots or edges

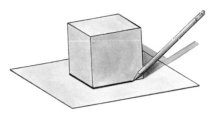

2. With the pencil, trace around the wood block on the tracing paper.

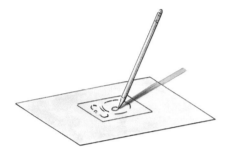

3. Inside the shape you drew, draw a stamp design, the simpler, the better. Or copy a design from the examples on page 11. Leave at least a ¹/₂ inch margin on all sides. Avoid tiny details. Make any letters at least ¹/₂ inch tall.

4. Darken all your lines with the pencil. Cut out the tracing.

5. Tape the tracing down onto the foam, covering all edges of the paper with tape, with the pencil markings facing the foam.

6. Use the flat side of the pencil or the wood block to rub firmly back and forth across the back of the paper. This transfers the pencil design to the foam.

7. Remove the paper. The design should appear backward on the foam.

8. On the foam, dig out any lines inside your design with the screwdriver, as shown. Cut out the outline of the design with the scissors

9. To make a stamp, use masking tape to stick the foam design to the bottom of the block. (Roll a few pieces of masking tape into cylinders with the sticky side facing out.) The penciled side should face out. No part of the foam should be wider than the block.

10. Brush a thin coat of paint over the foam. Clean your brush in the jar of water.

11. Press the stamp onto scrap paper. Lift it to check your design. If some lines didn't show up on the paper, cut deeper into the foam. First clean the foam with a damp paper towel, then unstick the foam, fix the design, and tape the foam back on the block.

12. Apply more paint and try again. To get a good print, press all corners down evenly and firmly, without moving the block on the paper. Then lift the stamp straight up.

13. Stamp once in one corner of each sheet of paper.

These are examples of British stamps used on paper. The Stamp Act taxed paper used for diplomas, newspapers, and other documents. Each sheet of paper had the price stamped in the corner, inside a special design. The stamped paper was shipped to the colonies from Britain, but patriots attacked or threatened the people who planned to sell it.

Mobcap

Boston: March 5, 1770

You and your sister have been visiting friends. As you leave, you see a mob of men and boys shouting at British soldiers.

"We did not send for you! We will not have you here!" yells one man. "We will drive you away!"

"Wretched rebels!" your sister mutters. "This is **treason**. And dangerous! These men are begging to be shot!"

A group of men push past you, roughly. Your sister stumbles, her cap falling to the icy ground. She reaches for it.

"Never mind your cap," you murmur. "Let's hurry home."

A group of colonists watch the Battle of Bunker Hill from rooftops in Boston.

1. With the pen, trace around the bowl onto the cloth. Cut out the circle.

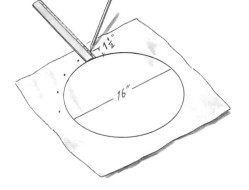

2. Using the ruler, draw a dot 1½ inches outside the circle's edge. Put a pen dot there. Repeat this step all around the circle, making 25 to 30 dots, all 1½ inches outside the circle. Connect the dots to make a larger circle.

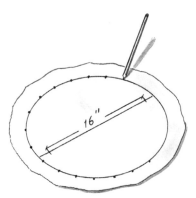

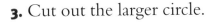

3. Cut out the larger circle.

4. Now make dots 1½ to 2 inches apart, on top of the inner circle, all the way around.

5. Choose one dot on the inner circle. Pinch up the fabric at the dot, making a fold. The fold should lie in the same direction as the circle's edge.

6. Cut a small slit (about ¼ to ½ inch long) across the fold. The direction of the slit should be from the edge of the inner circle toward the center of the circle.

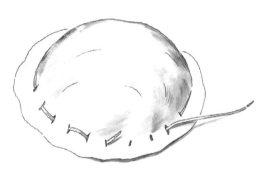

7. Repeat this step at every dot along the inner circle.

8. Thread the shoelace or ribbon in and out through all the slits. Make sure both ends come out on the same side of the cloth. (You might need to skip a slit.) Pull both ends to form a cap.

9. Holding both ends of the lace, try on the cap. Have a friend even out the ruffles and tie a neat bow in front.

Stewed Pears

You will need:

- 3 pears
- cutting board
- paring knife
- medium-sized pot with lid
- 2 whole cloves
- $1/2$ cup sugar
- piece of lemon peel about $1 1/2$ by 2 inches
- 1 cup unsweetened white grape juice
- water
- large spoon
- stove
- fork
- pot holder
- slotted spoon
- serving bowls

1. Get adult permission or help.

2. Wash your hands and the pears. Place the pears on the cutting board.

3. With the knife, cut the pears into quarters, the long way, and remove the cores.

4. Place the pears in the pot along with the cloves, sugar, lemon peel, and grape juice. Add enough water to just cover the pears. Stir with the large spoon.

5. Cook on medium heat until the mixture boils.

6. Turn the heat to low and cover the pot. Cook thirty minutes or until the pears are tender when poked with a fork. Stir occasionally.

7. Holding the pot handle with a pot holder, scoop up the pear pieces with the slotted spoon and put them in bowls to cool before serving.

General George Washington at the Battle of Princeton in January 1777. This and other battles drove the British from New Jersey.

3

The Patriots

The patriots believed that Americans should govern themselves. They wanted freedom from British rule. Famous patriots included George Washington, who led the **Continental Army**; Patrick Henry, who made a famous speech about liberty; Paul Revere, who rode to warn Americans that British soldiers were marching to Concord; and Thomas Jefferson, who authored the Declaration of Independence. Most colonists took the patriots' side.

African Americans had a special problem when they chose sides. Some patriot leaders favored slavery, especially in the South. The British, on the other hand, promised slaves freedom. Some African-American slaves fled to the British. But many others, slaves or free, fought bravely on the American side.

Many colonists belonged to groups called Sons of Liberty. These groups set up liberty poles in villages, where they sometimes met to discuss how they could break free from Britain. In some villages, flags flew from these poles. Liberty flags were usually red, and bore the word "Liberty" or "Union."

Liberty Flag
Concord, Massachusetts: April 19, 1775

You are standing outside your home, feeling angry. Inside, a British soldier is moving from room to room, banging open cupboards looking for hidden weapons and supplies. You know he won't find any. Your father told you that everything had already been moved to other towns.

Still, you are angry. "They've got no right to search our house!" you mutter to your brother.

"Did you hear they chopped down the town's **liberty flag**?" he whispers back. "I wish I was old enough to be a **minuteman**!"

You will need:

- plastic drop cloth
- pencil
- plain cloth (usually red for a Sons of Liberty flag), about 20 by 15 inches

- fabric paints or acrylic paints
- paper plate
- paintbrushes
- jar of water

- scissors
- duct tape
- 3-foot dowel or bamboo garden stake

1. Spread a plastic sheet to cover your work surface to protect it, since paint may soak through the flag.

2. With the pencil, sketch a design onto the cloth. Make sure you have enough room for all your letters. Leave 1 to 2 inches blank along the left edge, for the pole.

3. Pour or squeeze paints of different colors onto the paper plate. Do not try to squeeze fabric paint directly onto the flag.

4. Paint over the design you drew on the cloth. Clean the paintbrushes in the jar of water.

5. Let the flag dry completely. This may take one or more days.

6. Lay the flag face down on the table with the undecorated part hanging slightly off the edge of the work surface.

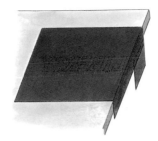

7. Cut a piece of duct tape several inches long. Starting at the top of the flag, lay the tape, sticky side down, lengthwise along the edge hanging off the work surface. Most of the tape's width should hang off the flag. Place another piece of duct tape next to the first. Continue until duct tape lies along the entire edge.

8. Turn the flag over so the tape is sticky side up. Place the flagpole carefully along the tape edge that is farthest from the flag. One inch of the flagpole should stick out above the tape. Roll the pole toward the flag, so the tape wraps around the pole. Stop when the flagpole touches the cloth.

9. Wave your flag with pride!

21

The Declaration of Independence is read to cheering colonists in Philadelphia, 1776.

Tricorn Hat

Philadelphia. July 8, 1776.

It is a warm, sunny day. You and your mother are standing outside the Statehouse. Around you, a crowd waits impatiently to hear the brand-new Declaration of Independence read aloud.

Your mother says, "Your uncle died fighting for this moment. He was in a battle near Boston. Some people didn't want free black men fighting for this country. He fought anyway, because he believed in freedom from Britain."

You grip her hand tightly. Just then, a voice begins to read: "When in the course of human events. . . ."

You will need:

- a helper
- tape measure
- white colored pencil
- 1 sheet of black poster board, 22 by 28 inches
- scissors

- bowl or pot lid about 16 inches across, to trace around
- stapler
- glue stick
- yellow or white plastic

(sold in craft or stationery stores) or electrical tape, 1/2 to 1 inch wide
- 1 sheet of black tissue paper, at least 15 inches on each side

Make the Crown

1. Have the helper measure all around your head where the edge of a hat would sit. Mark that length with a white pencil on the black poster board. Add 2 inches to the length. Cut a strip of poster board that long and 2 inches wide. Staple it into a ring, making a headband.

2. Put on the headband. Have the helper measure your head from the bottom of the headband in front (above your face), over your head, to the bottom of the headband in back.

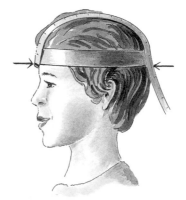

3. Cut a strip of poster board exactly that long and 2 inches wide. Call it strip A.

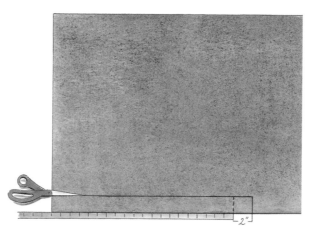

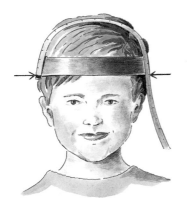

4. Now have the helper measure from the bottom of the headband over one ear, to the bottom of the headband over the other ear, going over the top of your head. Cut one more strip of poster board exactly this long and 2 inches wide. Call it strip B.

5. Take off the headband. Staple the ends of strip A where the front of your head and back of your head would be. Staple the ends of strip B above where your left ear and right ear would be. Strip B should cross strip A. Be sure each strip is level with the bottom of the headband at both ends. You should now have the oval-shaped crown of a hat with two strips crisscrossing it.

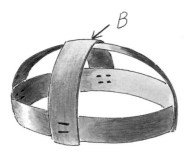

Make the Brim

1. Trace around the bowl or pot lid on the poster board. Cut out the circle.

2. Place the hat crown in the middle of the circle. Trace around it. Remove the crown. Draw four criss-crossing lines across the oval you just traced, as shown.

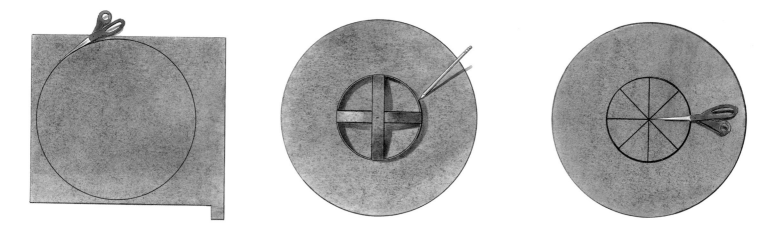

3. Cut along the crisscrossing lines, as shown, stopping and starting each at the edge of the oval. (At the start, you may need help.) This will make triangles.

4. Fold all the triangles back so they stand up. Cut off the points so the sticking-up shapes are about 1¹/₂ inches tall. This will be the hat brim.

5. Try to fit the hat crown inside the brim. You will probably need to cut the brim a bit between the standing shapes.

6. Staple the standing shapes to the outside of the headband. Make sure the sharp ends of each staple face outward, away from your head.

7. Fold one side of the brim up and staple it to the headband. Do this three times, once on each side, and once in back, making the brim sort of triangular.

8. Using the glue stick, put glue on the outside of the crisscrossed strips. Lay the tissue paper over the crisscrossed strips and press down on top of the glue. Trim the tissue-paper edges and tuck them in under the turned-up brim.

9. With the colored tape, neatly tape along the edge of the brim, all the way around, for decoration. The tape will show on top in some places and on the bottom in others.

A soldier on duty at Valley Forge. During the American Revolution, more soldiers died of illness than were killed by the enemy.

Medical Kit
Valley Forge, Pennsylvania: December 1777

You and your family are camped at Valley Forge where your father is in the Continental Army. He is lying in his tent, very hot and sick. The army doctor is checking him.

"This is **putrid fever**," says the doctor. "We'd best take him to the hospital at Yellow Springs. They will bleed him."

"Bleed him?" your mother says, her voice weak.

"Put **leeches** on his body to suck his blood. That's the usual treatment. It helps restore balance to his body so he'll get well."

You will need:

- plain brown cardboard box or shoe box painted brown
- pencil or pen
- cardboard backing from notepad, at least 8 x by 11 inches

- scissors
- aluminum foil
- Scotch tape
- stick-on label

- clean disposable coffee cup with plastic lid
- brown clay (any kind)
- piece of muslin cloth, at least 18 inches long and at least 4 inches wide

1. Use the box to store your medical equipment in.

2. Make a saw for cutting off wounded arms or legs. Copy the picture of the saw below onto the cardboard. Cut it out. Cut a piece of aluminum foil as long as the blade and two to three times as wide. Fold the foil neatly around the blade and tape it in place.

3. Make a leech jar. Write *leeches* in fancy handwriting and stick it on the cup. Inside the cup, place one or more fat worms made from clay. Be sure to make airholes in the lid with the scissor so your leeches can breathe. Ask an adult to help.

4. Make bandages. Cut or tear the cloth into long strips 2 to 4 inches wide. Roll them up neatly.

5. Make a bullet by rolling a small piece of aluminum foil into a ball. In revolutionary America, there were no medicines to put people to sleep during surgery. Soldiers bit a bullet to keep from biting their tongues in pain.

The British Army marching in formation.

4

The British

The British were fighting to keep control of the colonies. Under orders from King George III and the British **Parliament**, well-trained British troops fought against American farmers and craftsmen. The British fought in straight lines, following old-fashioned rules. Americans often shot from behind trees and walls, the way that Native Americans did.

At first the British thought winning the war would be easy. But the Americans fought well and got help from France and other European countries.

In the last great battle, the Americans and French defeated the British at Yorktown, Virginia, in 1781. It took two more years for the British to agree to end the war. In September 1783 the British and Americans signed the final peace agreements. America was then fully free of British rule.

British Flag

Cowpens, South Carolina: January 17, 1781

You are a member of the British Seventh **Regiment**. Your job is to carry the British flag into battle. You are carrying it proudly, even though you feel tired. You had to get up at 3:00 A.M. because your commander, Colonel Tarleton, was impatient to attack the Americans. You have slept for only four hours in the past two days.

Your regiment is very well trained. You have no doubt you will win this battle. Whatever happens, you want to be sure the flag is not captured.

The battle begins. The Americans are fighting much better than you thought they could. Suddenly American soldiers are coming from everywhere. They capture the flag!

You will need:

- scissors
- blue felt, about 9 by 12 inches
- red and white felt pieces, at least 8 by 8 inches
- white glue
- needle and thread, thin dowel (1/4 inch thick) 18 to 36 inches long, and duct tape, optional

1. Cut out red and white strips of felt to match the pattern below.

 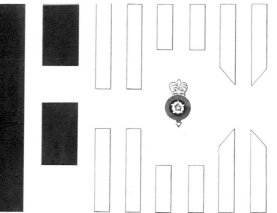

2. Lay the felt strips onto the blue background. Trim them as needed. Glue them down. It is OK to over-lap some pieces.

knot

GLUE

3. If you want your flag to be more secure, sew each piece on once glue dries. Tie a knot in a piece of thread. Thread the needle. Ask an adult to help you. Starting at the back of the flag, sew a row of stitches down the middle of a strip of felt. When you reach the end of a row, take three stitches backward, remove the needle, and trim the end of the thread. Repeat for the other strips.

4. If you plan to use a pole, stitch on the flag design. Otherwise the pieces may fall off.

5. To attach the flagpole, cut a strip of duct tape that equals the height of the flag (about 9 inches). Lay the flag face up with the duct tape, sticky side up, next to the left edge of the flag. Tuck about ¼ to ½ inch of the tape under the flag and press the felt down. Place the pole on the tape's left edge and roll it toward the flag until it meets the felt.

Drum
Yorktown, Virginia: October 17, 1781

You are a drummer for His Majesty's Army. The Battle of Yorktown has just ended. Your general, Cornwallis, has decided to surrender.

You march out of the town, beating a drum covered with black cloth. Around you, the American and French armies watch. Their faces look determined, excited, and eager.

When you arrived in the colonies, you had nothing but scorn for the Americans. Now, it seems, they might actually win—not just this battle, but independence.

Let them, you think. Let them have their new country.

All you want to do is go home.

You will need:

- tube-shaped oatmeal box, empty
- 1 sheet of construction paper, 12 by 18 inches
- pencil
- yardstick
- scissors
- 1 or more felt-tipped markers
- glue stick
- Scotch tape
- colored plastic or electrical tape, 1 inch wide
- shoelace, at least 36 inches long
- 2 new unsharpened pencils with erasers

1. Take off the box lid and save it.

2. Lay the box on top of the construction paper along the short side, as shown, with the bottom of the box exactly at the corner, as shown below.

3. With the pencil, make a dot on the paper at the top of the box.

4. Leaving the paper flat, roll the box to the other end of the paper. Keep the bottom of the box even with the bottom edge of the paper.

5. Make another dot where the top of the box touches the paper at the other end.

6. Remove the box. Lay the yardstick right below the two dots. Draw a straight line along the yardstick. Cut along the line.

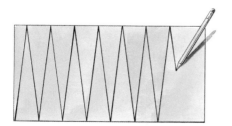

7. With the markers, draw zigzags (as shown) up and down on the paper.

8. Turn the paper over and spread glue on the back. Leave the paper glue side up.

9. Lay the box on top of the paper, just as you did in step 2.

10. Using the Scotch tape, tape the end of the paper to the box. Carefully roll the box along the glue-covered paper, keeping it as straight as possible.

11. Tape the other right edge of the paper to the paper-covered drum.

12. Once the glue is dry, put the lid back on.

13. Neatly unroll plastic tape all the way around the edge of the box bottom, for decoration.

14. Measure the shoelace by placing it over your shoulder and on a slant across your chest is in the last drawing. It should hang a few inches below your waist front and back. Trim if it is too long. Then take off the shoelace.

15. Scotch tape the ends of the shoelace to either side of the top of the box. The shoelace tips should point down.

16. Unroll plastic tape along the top edge of the box lid, going right over the taped-down shoelace tips.

17. Sling the drum over your head and shoulder and tap out a rhythm on the drum top with the eraser ends of the pencils.

Benjamin Franklin, Thomas Jefferson, John Adams, Robert Livingston, and Roger Sherman (shown from left to right) writing the Declaration of Independence.

Epilogue

The American Revolution officially ended on September 3, 1783.

In 1787, **delegates** to the **Continental Congress** in Philadelphia approved the **Constitution** of the United States. The next year it became law. That was the first time a country adopted a plan for a government of the people, by the people, and for the people.

Today the original document, yellowed with age, is in the National **Archives** in Washington, D.C.

George Washington and other patriots at the signing of the United States Constitution

Make a Copy of the Constitution

You will need:

- oven
- sheet of plain unlined paper
- cookie sheet or baking dish with sides, large enough to hold the paper laid flat
- pen
- 1 cup of plain coffee or strong black tea, cooled
- oven
- pot holders
- trivet

1. Get adult permission or help. Set the oven to 200° Farenheit, or as low as possible.

2. Place the paper flat in the pan.

3. Slowly pour just enough tea or coffee over the paper to cover it completely.

4. Place the pan in the oven. Bake for eight to ten minutes or until all the liquid is gone.

5. Remove the pan with pot holders and let it cool on the trivet.

6. Remove the paper. Once it is completely dry, using your best handwriting, copy onto it the preamble to the Constitution:

We the People of the United States, in Order to form a more perfect Union, establish Justice, insure domestic Tranquility, provide for the common defence, promote the general Welfare, and secure the Blessings of Liberty to ourselves and our Posterity, do ordain and establish this Constitution for the United States of America.

Glossary

archives: A place to store a collection of important papers.

colonies: Groups of people who leave their own country and settle in a distant land but are ruled by their home country; the lands settled by this group of people.

Constitution: A document that lays out a government's organization, powers, duties, and principles.

Continental Army: American soldiers in the Revolutionary War.

Continental Congress: A meeting of delegates from the thirteen colonies.

delegates: People chosen to represent a group of people at a meeting.

epilogue: The final section of a book, which tells what happened later.

leeches: Worms that suck blood.

liberty flag: A flag hung on a liberty pole. Usually red, with the word *liberty* or *union*.

loyalist: A colonist who wanted the British to continue ruling America. They were also called Tories.

minuteman: A member of a group of men ready to defend their town or country at a moment's notice.

Parliament: The part of the British government that votes on laws.

patriot: A colonist who supported American freedom from Britain.

putrid fever: The old-fashioned name for either typhus (a disease spread by lice) or another disease called typhoid fever. Both caused a fever and a rash, and could kill. Early Americans could not tell them apart.

Glossary

regiment: Part of an army.

Stamp Act: One way the British taxed the American colonists, by ordering them to pay for special stamped paper to use in writing many kinds of documents.

tarred and feathered: Coated with hot tar and covered with feathers; a form of punishment.

Tories: see *loyalist*

treason: Betraying the government.

Find Out More

Books

Adler, David. *Heroes of the Revolution.* New York: Holiday House, 2003.

Davis, Burke. *Black Heroes of the American Revolution.* San Diego: Harcourt Brace, 1976.

Fritz, Jean. *Shh! We're Writing the Constitution.* New York: G. P. Putnam's Sons, 1987.

Kirkpatrick, Katherine. *Redcoats and Petticoats.* New York: Holiday House, 1999.

Masoff, Joy. *American Revolution: 1700–1800.* New York: Scholastic Reference, 2000.

Miller, Brandon Marie. *Growing Up in Revolution and the New Nation: 1775–1800.* Minneapolis: Lerner Publications, 2003.

Web Sites:

The American Revolution: Lighting Freedom's Flame
www.nps.gov/revwar

Archiving Early America
www.earlyamerica.com

Colonial Williamsburg, Virginia
www.colonialwilliamsburg.org/

Liberty! The American Revolution (from the 1997 PBS series)
www.pbs.org/ktca/liberty/

Metric Conversion Chart

You can use the chart below to convert from U. S. measurements to the metric system.

Weight
1 ounce = 28 grams
½ pound (8 ounces) = 227 grams
1 pound = .45 kilogram
2.2 pounds = 1 kilogram

Liquid volume
1 teaspoon = 5 milliliters
1 tablespoon = 15 milliliters
1 fluid ounce = 30 milliliters
1 cup = 240 milliliters (.24 liter)
1 pint = 480 milliliters (.48 liter)
1 quart = .95 liter

Length
¼ inch = .6 centimeter
½ inch = 1.27 centimeters
1 inch = 2.54 centimeters

Temperature
100°F = 40°C
110°F = 45°C
350°F = 180°C
375°F = 190°C
400°F = 200°C
425°F = 220°C
450°F = 235°C

About the Author

Marian Broida has a special interest in hands-on history for children. Growing up near George Washington's home in Mount Vernon, Virginia, Ms. Broida spent much of her childhood pretending she lived in colonial America. She has written six other titles for the Hands-On History series. In addition to children's activity books, she writes books for adults on health care topics and occasionally works as a nurse. Ms. Broida lives in Decatur, Georgia.

Index